TREETOP TWINS
WILDERNESS ADVENTURES

The Twins Help a
Pink Dolphin

Cressida Cowell

Hodder
Children's
Books

There are seven purple fish in this
book. Can you find them all?

The water swished and swirled as winds rippled its surface and creatures moved beneath. The Treetop family have transformed

their time machine into a boat and they have travelled, not back in time, but far, far away, to the Amazon River in South America.

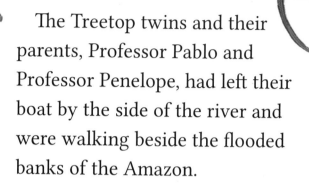

The Treetop twins and their parents, Professor Pablo and Professor Penelope, had left their boat by the side of the river and were walking beside the flooded banks of the Amazon.

Asha was looking for jaguars. Alfie was looking for piranhas. Ted was looking for caimans. And Tulip was looking for unicorns.

Tulip spotted a flash of pink in the brown water.

'Look!' cried Tulip. 'That must be a unicorn! It's pink!'

'Unicorns aren't pink!' said Ted. 'And more importantly, unicorns aren't real...'

'Oh no, you're right,' said a disappointed Tulip as she got a closer look at the pink animal. 'It's not a unicorn, it's a dolphin.'

'But dolphins aren't pink either!' protested Ted.

'These are a very special kind of dolphin,' explained Professor Pablo. 'The Amazon river dolphin.'

'They have lots of teeth,' said Asha, making notes in her notebook.

'That's because they eat crabs and turtles, as well as fish,' said Professor Penelope. 'They're not picky eaters!'

'Neither am I,' grinned Alfie. 'I'll eat anything!'

More dolphins appeared and they were in a playful mood.

They swam in circles around each other. One of them had some river weed in its mouth, and it slapped the weed on the surface of the water. Another had a stick between its teeth, and it swirled around,

waving the stick importantly.

'What are they doing?' asked Asha.

'The male dolphins are trying to make friends with the female dolphins,' said Alfie.

The female dolphin didn't look very interested. She swam off.

'She's looking for food because she's hungry,' said Asha.

'Just like me!' said Alfie.

'How can she see anything in the water?' asked Ted. 'It's so muddy.'

'Dolphins hunt using echolocation,' explained Professor Penelope. 'They make lots of clicks and whistles, and the sounds bounce back, telling them where everything is.'

Asha was drawing pictures in her notebook when a noise from above caught her attention. Looking up, she saw a little bird doing dance moves on a branch to make friends with a female bird.

SQUAAAWK!

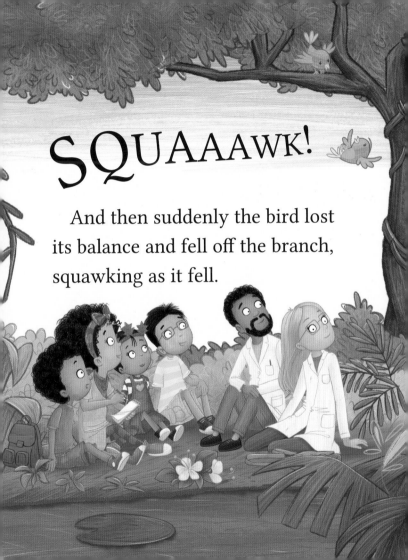

And then suddenly the bird lost its balance and fell off the branch, squawking as it fell.

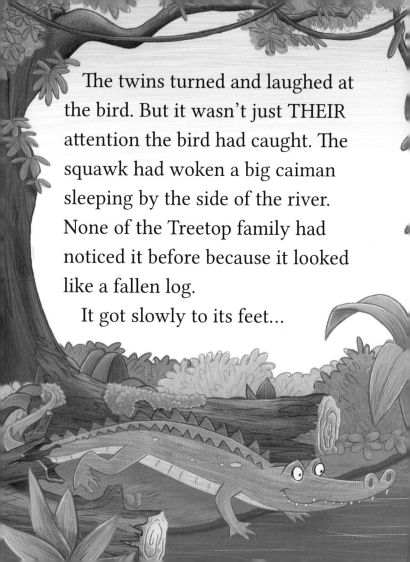

The twins turned and laughed at the bird. But it wasn't just THEIR attention the bird had caught. The squawk had woken a big caiman sleeping by the side of the river. None of the Treetop family had noticed it before because it looked like a fallen log.

It got slowly to its feet...

And slipped into the water!

'Oh no, it's heading for the female pink dolphin!' said Ted.

'I wouldn't worry,' said Professor Pablo. 'Dolphins are a lot cleverer than caimans – she'll be fine.'

But Ted wasn't taking any chances.

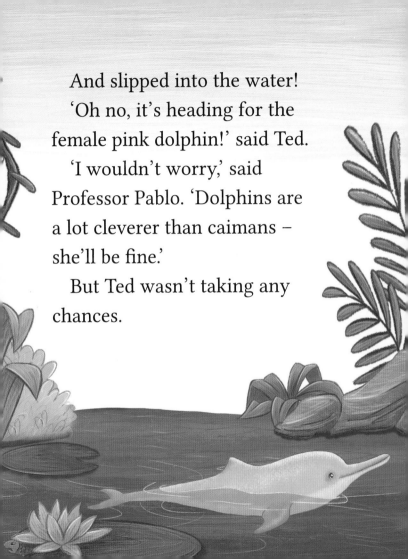

He fetched one of the paddles from their boat and bashed it as hard as he could against the bottom of the riverbed.

BASH! BASH! BASH! went the paddle.

SPLASH! SPLASH! SPLASH! went the water.

Sure enough, the female pink dolphin heard the noise – spotted the caiman – and immediately swam off down the river before the caiman got too close.

'Phew!' said Professor Pablo.

'Well done, Ted! Now we'd better get back in our boat and head off before the caiman swims back this way again!'

Night-time in the Amazon rainforest.

The Treetop family were gathered around the campfire. Ted had tied his T-shirt around his head so he couldn't see where he was going and he was making strange whistling noises.

'What are you doing, Ted?' asked Asha.

'I'm going to be the first human being to find my supper by echolocation,' boasted Ted.

'Maybe,' said Asha, unimpressed. 'But in the meantime, you've just trodden on your sandwich.'

'Don't worry, I'LL eat it!' said Alfie.

Alfie wasn't a picky eater.

He really would eat anything.

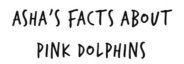

ASHA'S FACTS ABOUT PINK DOLPHINS

Pink dolphins hunt using echolocation.

Amazon river dolphins are also known as pink dolphins, because of their pink bodies.

The male pink dolphin uses stones and sticks and weeds to attract the female dolphin's attention.